THE CATS OF
Mrs. Calamari

Handle w/ Care

↑ This side up

by John Stadler

ORCHARD BOOKS

NEW YORK

Orchard Books, 95 Madison Avenue, New York, NY 10016

Manufactured in the United States of America
Printed by Barton Press, Inc.
Bound by Horowitz/Rae
Book design by Jennifer Campbell

10   9   8   7   6   5   4   3   2   1

The text of this book is set in 18 point Esprit.
The illustrations are ink line and watercolor reproduced in full color.

Library of Congress Cataloging-in-Publication Data
Stadler, John.
The cats of Mrs. Calamari / by John Stadler.
p.   cm.
"A Richard Jackson book"—Half t.p.

Summary: Mrs. Calamari's new landlord tells her that no cats will
be allowed starting Sunday, thus beginning a week of trickery and
amusing deception, ending in a happy surprise.

ISBN 0-531-30020-X. — ISBN 0-531-33020-6 (lib. bdg.)
[1. Cats—Fiction.   2. Apartment houses—Fiction.
3. Landlord and tenant—Fiction.   4. Humorous stories.]   I. Title.
PZ7.S77575Caw   1997   [E]—dc20   96-42283

To my father:
one cool cat

On a lovely spring Monday, Mrs. Calamari began her week by moving into a fine new apartment.

During Tuesday's dinner, there was a knock at the door.

"I am the new owner of the building,
Everett T. Gangplank," the man said.
"And this is my dog, Potato."
"Pleased to meet you," said Mrs. Calamari.

"Ah, Mrs. Calamari . . . I have lost my glasses,
but I thought I saw some cats walk in here yesterday.
I cannot stand cats," Mr. Gangplank said.
"And Potato does not like them either. Do you have
any cats, Mrs. Calamari?"

"Cats?" she asked. "Well, before I moved here
I had more cats than I could count, but now all I have
are these little statues that I keep on the shelf."

"Heavens!" said Mr. Gangplank. "They look so real. But
in my building there will be no cats allowed as of Sunday.
All cats must be out, out, out . . . or something will happen."

On Wednesday, Mrs. Calamari heard a noise
outside her window.
"Mr. Gangplank!" she exclaimed. "What are you
and Potato doing out there?"
"Oh, just hanging around," he said. "Are you sure
there aren't any cats in your apartment?"

"Cats? Of course not," Mrs. Calamari said
as she lowered the shade.

Before long there was a knocking.
"We are stuck," Mr. Gangplank said.
"You're in luck," said Mrs. Calamari. "My cousins are visiting from Texas. They can help you."

Soon Potato and Mr. Gangplank were safely inside.
"Your cousins have tails and look like cats!"
Mr. Gangplank remarked.

"Really?" said Mrs. Calamari. "I never noticed."
"Just wait until I find my glasses!" Mr. Gangplank said.
"And remember, all cats must be out, out, out
by Sunday . . . or something will happen."

Thursday morning, Mr. Gangplank saw
Mrs. Calamari walking with a group of short,
uniformed figures on the street.
"Who are *they?*" he asked.

"These are my nieces and nephews from the air force.
They are visiting for my birthday tomorrow."
"Why, tomorrow is *my* birthday too!" Mr. Gangplank cried.
"Happy birthday!" said Mrs. Calamari before moving on.

Mr. Gangplank and Potato stopped their work in front of the building. "Didn't those nieces and nephews remind you of cats, Potato?" Mr. Gangplank asked. "If we stay here, maybe we can get another look at them coming back." They waited and waited.

But Mr. Gangplank fell asleep.

"Goodness!" he cried when he awoke.
"Where did all these presents come from?"
Potato did his best to explain.

On Friday, Mr. Gangplank had an idea.
"Potato," he said, "I have invited Mrs. Calamari
and her relatives over for a birthday party. I will dress up
as a mouse. Cats cannot stand mice.
If Mrs. Calamari's relatives don't like me,
then they are not relatives. They are cats!"

Soon there was a knock at his door.

"Potato!" Mrs. Calamari said from the hallway.

"What are you doing with that kangaroo?"

"I am not a kangaroo," said Mr. Gangplank.

"I am a mouse! I want to see if your relatives are really cats."

"Well, my relatives *love* kangaroos," said Mrs. Calamari as they entered, "especially my grandchildren. They flew in from Kalamazoo and are staying for my birthday."

"Oh!" said Mr. Gangplank.

He was very popular.

"Wait! I nearly forgot," said Mr. Gangplank
as he ran to the kitchen. "I am baking you a cake."

Smoke filled the room.
"Mrs. Calamari?" Mr. Gangplank called.
"Do you like your cake well done?"

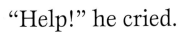

"Help!" he cried.

They carried Mr. Gangplank to safety
and quickly put out the fire.

"Look! A kangaroo!" people called from the street.

Saturday morning, Mr. Gangplank called to Mrs. Calamari and her relatives in the hallway.

"Quick. Get in!" he cried, pointing to the elevator.

"Why?" asked Mrs. Calamari.

"To celebrate! After today all the cats in my building will be out, out, out. And since you and your relatives have been so kind to us, Potato and I want to drive you someplace special. My car is right downstairs."

"Lovely," said Mrs. Calamari. "But my aunts and uncles are here, too, from Ohio."

"Bring them along," he said. "Bring them *all!*"

"Pizzas for everyone!" Mr. Gangplank hollered
as they hit the beach.

"There's something I must tell you,"
Mrs. Calamari said. "It has to do with cats."
"Wait!" Mr. Gangplank said. "Look what I found.
My glasses! They must have been in this pocket
the whole time!"

He was about to put them on when the lifeguard approached.

"Cats are not allowed!" the lifeguard shouted.

"Get them *off the beach* or else!"

"Cats?" Mr. Gangplank asked. "Where?"

"You had better put on your glasses, Mr. Gangplank," said Mrs. Calamari.

Mr. Gangplank turned slowly and put his glasses on.
He was speechless.

He took a deep breath. After a moment he turned
toward the lifeguard and said, "My dear sir,
you must be mistaken. *You* may see cats before you,
but *I* do not see cats. What I see is my family!
Now leave us alone . . . or something will happen!"

On Sunday, something did happen! Mrs. Calamari and Mr. Gangplank ended the week with a wedding. Only their closest relatives attended.